Brothers Grimm

The Bremen Musicians

Illustrations of O. Kiriyenko

Translated by Victor Voloshchuk

As it is known, old age does not bring joy. Weakened and unable to work, the donkey has been expelled from the courtyard, where he worked hard for many years. In order not to starve to death, he decided to go to Bremen and become a musician. On the way he meets several animals who consider that his idea is a splendid one and joins him. But night fell, and the animals settled down for the night in the forest. And what happened next, you can learn by reading this book.

Many years ago, a miller lived in a village. And he had a donkey, a good one, smart and strong.

The donkey worked for a long time at the mill: he dragged bags of flour on his back — and finally he got old. He weakened and was no longer suitable for work. And his master drove him out of the court-yard.

The donkey mourned some time and decided to go to Bremen to become a town musician there.

He went along the road and coached his voice, roaring loud.

Suddenly, he saw a dog, which was lying on the road and breathing heavily.

"Why are you so out of breath?" asked the donkey.

"I'm tired. I ran for a long time."

"Why did you run like that?"

"I lived with a hunter a long time. I ran around the fields and swamps and brought to him the game, which he had shot. But now I became old, and my master decided to kill me, so I ran away from him, but I don't know what to do next."

"Come with me to Bremen, we will become the musicians there. You will sing and beat the drum, and I will play the guitar."

And they went together to Bremen.

They walked and walked, and suddenly they saw: there was a cat sitting on the road, a sad one, un- happy.

"Why are you so sad?" they asked him.

"I lived with my mistress a long time, I caught rats and mice. And now I became old, and she wanted to drown me in a river. I ran away from home."

"Come with us to Bremen; we will become town musicians there. You will sing and play the violin."

And they went on together.

They walked ahead and trained their voices, each of them was singing his own song: the donkey shouted, the dog barked and the cat meowed.

After some time, they walked past a courtyard and saw: a rooster was sitting on the gate and scream-ing at the top of his neck: "Doodle-do!"

"Why are you screaming? Maybe someone offended you?" they asked.

"Tomorrow morning the guests will come to my hosts, and now they are going to kill and cook me. What should I do?"

The donkey replied:

"Come with us to Bremen, and we all will become the street singers."

And they went on together.

On the road, they trained their voices again: the donkey shouted, the dog barked, the cat meowed and the rooster crowed.

They walked and walked ahead until the night fell. Then the donkey, the dog and the cat lay down under an oak tree and the rooster flew up onto a branch and began to look around.

He looked and looked, and suddenly saw that a light was shining nearby.

"I see the light!" cried the rooster.

"We need to find out what kind of light it is. Maybe there's a house nearby."

Soon they came to a clearing and saw a hut with a lighted window.

The donkey went up to the hut and looked through the window.

"What do you see there?"

"The robbers are sitting at the table, eating and drinking."

"Oh, how hungry I am!" said the dog.

"How would we expel the robbers from hut?"

They thought and thought, and finally came up.

The donkey quietly put his front legs on the window-sill, the dog climbed onto his back, the cat jumped onto the dog's back, and the rooster flew up onto the cat's head. And all they at once screamed — everyone in his own way.

They screamed and burst through the window into the room. The robbers got scared and fled into the forest.

The friends sat around the table and began to dinner.

They ate and drank, and went to sleep. The donkey sprawled on the hay in the yard, the dog lay down in front of the kitchen door, the cat curled up in a ball on the stove, and the rooster climbed onto the gate.

And the robbers were sitting in the forest and looking at their hut. They saw: a light in the window went out.

Then they sent one robber to see what was happen-
ing in the hut.

He went to the hut, opened the door and entered the kitchen; he looked and saw: on the stove two lights were burning. He poked a splinter into the light and jabbed into the cat's eye.

The cat got angry, jumped up, snorted, hissed and pawed the robber with his paw.

The robber ran out the door. And then the dog grabbed his leg.

The robber rushed into the yard. And there a donkey attacked him.

The robber ran to the gate. And from the gate the
rooster cried out: "Doodle-do!"

The robber rushed at full speed into the forest.

He came to his comrades and said:

"It's the trouble! Terrible giants settled in our hut. One of them scratched my whole face with a spear, the second cut my leg with a knife, the third hit me on the back with a club, and the fourth shouted after me: 'Hold the thief!'"

The robbers were scared to death and left this forest forever.

And the Bremen musicians, the donkey, the dog, the cat and the rooster, remained to live in their hut.

See also:

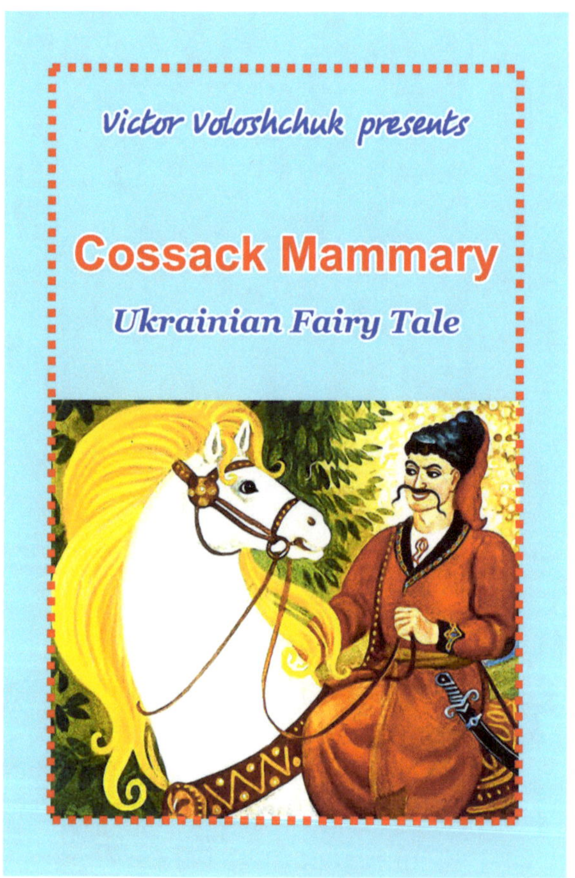

A kind and generous man named Mammary served for the landlord twenty-five years, but earned only three copper coins. So he decided to go into the world to look at the people and to search happiness. This fairy tale tells the story of all his adventures, and about how it ended.